MW00929119

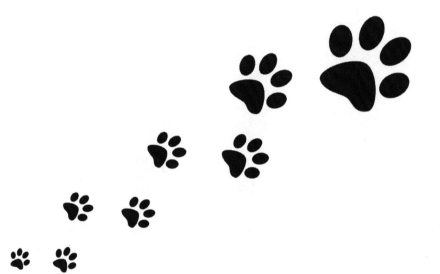

# Ellie Adventure Picking Out Puppies

# Ellie Adventure

## Picking Out Puppies

*To Nicholas,*
*I hope you enjoy the book!*
*Keep reading!*

*Colleen Dougherty*
*2017*

## Colleen Dougherty

Five Pad Publishing

Chandler, AZ

**Copyright 2015 © Colleen Dougherty**

All rights reserved.

Please do not use any part of this book or reproduce any part of this book without written permission from Colleen Dougherty. You may quote parts of the book for use in reviews of "Ellie Adventure Picking Out Puppies" or for use in articles. Elementary school students and teachers may use this book for any educational purpose. Copying the work in its entirety is forbidden.

This is a work of fiction. Names, characters, places, and incidents are either the product of the author's imagination or are used fictitiously. Any resemblance to actual persons, living or dead, events or locales is entirely coincidental.

Library of Congress Control Number: 2015909089
Createspace Independent Publishing Platform, North Charleston, SC
ISBN-13: 978-1511780643
ISBN-10: 1511780649
Printed in the United States of America
This first edition published by arrangement with Five Pad Publishing, Chandler, Arizona.
Skippy and Snickerdoodle illustrations by former Disney illustrator, John Ewing.
All other illustrations completed with vector art.
Cover by Dean Dougherty

For my dad, Bill Keating, for always encouraging me to write.

# Ellie Adventure

## Picking Out Puppies

### By: Colleen Dougherty

Contents

# Chapter One

## Stink Eye

The best thing about my birthdays, 'sides all the presents, is blowing out my candles, 'cause I get to make a wish! Every year I wish for the same thing.

I wish for a puppy!

When my birthday comes, I'll be six. Finally, my wish for a puppy is gonna come true 'cause Mommy and Daddy said that when I turn six I finally get my very own puppy!

My two friends at Dorsett Elementary, Lori and Dana, keep saying they want ponies.

I think that maybe it's 'cause they already have dogs so they probably just forgot how exciting it is to have a puppy. When I get mine, I'll have them over so they can remember.

"You can't ride a puppy, silly," Lori said, as she twirled her

hair between her fingers.

We were waiting to go outside for recess.

Recess is when you get to play for twenty minutes instead of learnin'.

It's my favoritest part of the school day 'cause I get to spend time with my friends, and Lori and Dana are my best friends.

We're best friends forever and ever.

I only have two best friends, and that's it...well, Julie and Lynne are best friends too! Of course, Shelly is a best friend and my bestie Karen, but that's it for best friends. I do have another best friend whose name is Julie too, so I have two best friends named Julie.

That's it for best friends. Well, actually, Cheyenne, Tyler,

Chelsea, Kelly and Joey are best friends too. Wait! I can't forget about Kathy, Sara, Emma, Clair, Susan and Beth 'cause they are, for sure, best friends too. I guess you can never have too many best friends!

"You can't feed a puppy carrots," Dana said. "Just get a pony and we'll have them all at the same stable so we can go there together. We'll have so much fun brushing their manes and tails and riding them."

"Yeah, and they'll be best friends, just like us!" Lori said, all giggly like. "Instead of being BFF's, best friends forever, they'll be BPF's, best ponies forever."

"Ponies need best friends too!" Dane said as we started to walk out to the playground.

I call her Dane when Dana is just too much to say.

"I'll get a brown one with a dark brown mane and dark brown tail," Dana said. "Lori wants a white one and you can get a spotted one."

"I don't want a spotted one," I tell her, but she's already

3

making plans, so I bet she doesn't even hear me. "I want a puppy."

"If you get a puppy then we won't have ponies at the same stable. Then they won't be best friends like we are," Lori said. "We want to get the same riding outfits for horse shows. You have to have a pony so you can do that too, Ellie."

"Yeah, you need to get with the program, Ellie," Dana said. "Just get the pony first and then you can get a puppy later."

We walked over to the swing sets 'cause it's more fun to talk when you're swinging on the swing sets. Tommy was already there having fun!

Lori sat down on the ground to wait for her turn and said, "You know they're fun to ride, right?"

"Well, everybody knows that!" I told her 'cause she needed reminding.

"Oh! Ponies love carrots!" Dana shouted. "You hate carrots, Ellie! That is so perfect."

"Huh?" I said, 'cause she wasn't making any sense.

"You *don't like* carrots. Ponies *like* carrots. You *have* to eat them at dinner. Get it?" she said, as she sat down next to Lori.

"Nope, not even a little bit," I told her.

Dana is usually a smarty, but she's not making any sense.

"If you had a pony you could give it your carrots instead of eating them," she told me.

"Oh!" I said, all smiley 'cause this was getting to be good news for me! Then I thought of something. "How am I supposed to get the carrots to that pony while we're having dinner?"

I got on the swing next to Tommy and started swinging.

"It's easy. You just teach him how to lay down under the table," Lori said, as she pulled a piece of grass out of the ground and tried to balance it across the bridge of her nose.

"I don't know...it's not a very big table," I told her as my swing got higher and higher. "I could just barely get my scooter under the table. Mommy says it's 'cause scooters aren't supposed to go under tables. She says scooters are meant to go in the garage, but I say that's just silly 'cause

6

I'm gonna be riding it in the house, so why go back and forth to the garage?"

That's just silly!

"Toss it to him when your parents aren't looking," Dana said, as she blew the piece of grass off Lori's nose.

"Wait a minute...don't puppies like carrots?" I asked as I slowed my swing down.

"Oh, well I guess maybe...yeah, I guess they would!" Dana said, and she started laughing like someone was tickling her toes or something! "I just know, for sure, that ponies like carrots."

"Those ponies are so smelly, and you can't keep them in your room and I, for sure, want a pet that can stay in my room. I'm getting a puppy," I told them.

"You're gonna keep that puppy in your room all the time?" Dana asked. "It's gonna get stinky in there."

"Momma said I can have that puppy in my room as long as it doesn't go potty in there. She said that it would be a big ol' mess and 'sides she says my carpet can't take any more devastation," I told them.

"What's 'devastation'?" Dana asked as she sat down on the swing after Tommy left to go on the slide.

"I think it has something to do with paint," I told them.

"I don't think it does, Ellie," Lori said as she walked over to the swings.

"Well, this one time I decided to paint my bedroom. Now I know I shouldn't do that without Mommy saying I can first 'cause painting's hard, and 'sides, what was I thinking doing something like that without asking?" I told them, as I

got off my swing.

"Oh no, did you get in trouble?" Lori asked as she sat down next to Dana on the swing set.

"Well, I got more paint on the carpet than I did on the wall, at least that's what Mommy told Daddy. So, I think 'devastation' has to do with painting...or crying 'cause Mommy was doing that too. I don't know, but it doesn't matter 'cause I got it all figured out," I told her.

H is for horse.

"What have you got figured out?" Lori asked. "How to get the paint on the wall instead of the carpet?"

"No, silly!" I told her. "I figured out how to not let that puppy make a big ol' mess in my bedroom. I'll just take it outside first!"

"Sounds like a good plan, Ellie," Dana said, as she kicked the gravel under her swing.

"I've been using my noodle," I said, tapping the side of my head.

"What about riding it or braiding its tail?" Lori asked. "You can't do that with a puppy."

"She can always just get a tall puppy with hair long enough to braid," Dana told her.

"No, that's crazy!" Lori said, and she started laughing. She must have caught the giggles from Dana. "You can't go to a horse show with a puppy. You have to have a pony."

"Don't you need a horse to go to a horse show?" I asked her, 'cause now she had me all confused.

"No, they let you bring ponies in 'cause they are cousins of horses, and it's family, so family is allowed," Lori told me.

I have such smarty-pants friends.

"Well, you can just ride double with one of us and your puppy will be the stable dog who is best friends with the ponies," Dana said, as she jumped off her swing.

See what I mean about smarty-pants friends?


My name is Ellie Maureen Carmichael, but no one calls me all that except for my mommy, and she only uses all of my names when I'm being naughty.

Momma mostly just calls me Ellie. Well, except when she calls me sweet pea or pumpkin or some other vegetable.

She says those are nicknames she uses 'cause she loves me, but I say it just makes me hungry.

In thirteen days, it will be my birthday, and I'll be six! I've been waiting my whole life to turn six, 'cause Momma said I could get a puppy when I turn six!

Mommy also said she doesn't know what she was thinking, which is just silly 'cause she was thinking of getting me a puppy!

It's just hard waiting another thirteen days.

I try to find things to do so I won't think about it, but it's not working. I'm just always thinking about getting that puppy.

There are books to read in my bedroom, but they are mostly books about, you guessed it, puppies. Even my coloring books are full of puppies!

Momma lets me help her cook dinner, and I help with the dishes, but the whole time I'm still thinking about puppies.

My mind just can't help it.

I just know we're going to have so much fun once the puppy gets here! I'm going to take that puppy for walks every day, give it baths every Saturday, and brush it every night before I go to bed.

I'll have a puppy bed for him in my room so after he goes outside to go potty, he can come inside and sleep with me.

He'll be so happy that all he'll want to do is wag his tail and give me puppy kisses!

With all the excitement, I decide that maybe we shouldn't wait thirteen days to start looking for my new puppy.

"There's no better time than the present," Daddy says, so I decided to let Momma in on it.

"Momma, maybe we should go the puppy store and start looking at them puppies," I tell her, but she doesn't answer.

"Mommmmmmmaaaaaa!" I yell as I walk around the house looking for her.

She's in her office talking on her phone, so I ask her again except this time I raise my voice and follow her from room to room to be sure she can hear me.

"Momma! Let's go to the puppy store and look for my puppy!" I tell her again, but I make sure I use my outside voice 'cause this situation calls for it.

She turns around and gives me the stink eye.

The stink eye is when Momma squints her eyes real small-like and makes her mouth real-tight like.

I think it's code for "be quiet" or "knock it off," but I know it means to stop doing whatever I'm doing.

It's parent sign language, I think.

I know she wants me to be quiet right now. I just keep thinking about what Daddy says, "Ask, and you shall receive," and I always try to listen to Daddy, so I cross my fingers and try one more time.

"Momma! I want my puppy, please!" I yelled as loud as my voice would come out of my body.

Momma shushed me, ran into her office and shut the door real loud.

I'm going to have to ask Daddy about that "Ask, and you shall receive" business 'cause it's not working for me.

Either Daddy forgot to tell Mommy about it or I'm just not doing it right.

D is for dog.

## Chapter Two

### On Second Thought

Today is Saturday, which always means I don't have to go to school.

I don't go to school on Sunday either.

Momma says that Saturday and Sunday are called the weekend. I don't know about that, but I do know that this is my favoritest Saturday so far in my whole life 'cause today Momma said we could drive over to the mall and look at them puppies!

Just thinking about it makes it hard to do anything with my mouth but smile with it!

She says we can get an idea of what kind of puppy we want to bring home.

I've got lots of ideas about what kind of puppy we should adopt! We've been reading books about puppies for as long as Mommy's been reading to me, so I really like them all.

I'm so excited that I can't even eat my cereal this morning. I just look at those floaty marshmellas and tap them with my spoon.

"Eat up, Ellie," Momma tells me. "You need to finish your cereal before we leave for the mall."

That makes me want to eat lightning-fast, so I hurry up with my cereal, drink my juice, and slam my cup down on the kitchen table.

"Done!" I tell Momma, as I wipe my mouth on the back of my sleeve.

J is for juice.

"Ellie, use a napkin! Please bring your dishes over to the sink and then get your shoes on," Momma said as she grabbed her keys. "Don't forget, Ellie, we're just looking at the puppies today and won't be taking any of them home with us. When it's time, we'll be going to the dog pound or a rescue group and adopting a puppy that needs a good home," Momma told me.

"Okay, Momma!" I shout, 'cause when I'm excited I always shout.

I don't have a volume knob, but Mommy and Daddy said they wish I did.

Even though they are grown-ups, they are still so silly sometimes…a volume knob, how silly!

We drive to the mall in our blue van. It takes five songs on the radio to get there.

Looking out the window, I see people walking their dogs. There is a mom walking a tiny dog. He'd be cute wearing a sweater!

"Hey Momma! We have to buy clothes for our puppy when we get one, okay? Can we buy clothes for our puppy? I just saw a little dog that would be so cute in a sweater! I bet he'd wear one if he had one!" I told her, as I bounced up and down in my car seat.

Mommy looked back in her rearview mirror and laughed. She didn't say anything 'cause I guess she was thinking about a dog wearing clothes!

"Look Mommy! There is a mom that is walking one… two…three…four…five…six dogs! She is walking six dogs all at the same time!" I told her.

Mommy said that the lady must be a dog walker, and I think Momma's right since that lady is walking all them dogs. I guess if she were running with them she'd be a dog runner.

It's crazy, but Momma says that busy people probably pay that lady to take their dogs for a walk for them.

Who wouldn't want to take their dog for a walk? That's just crazy!

Once we get to the parking lot I can see those big mall

doors, and it made me smile inside 'cause I knew there were puppies in that place! Mommy couldn't get me out of my car seat fast enough!

"Hey Momma, what if we see a puppy that looks like it needs a new home? We can bring it to our house if it seems like it needs a new home, right Momma?" I said as my feet start to skip without me even knowing they were going to skip!

"No dear, this is just to look. Our dog will be coming from the dog pound or a rescue group. Maybe this wasn't a good idea," she said as she locked the van.

After Mommy said that, she did something crazy.

She stopped right outside those big mall doors instead of walking in!

"Maybe I've made a mistake. Let's go get ice cream and make an appointment to go to the dog pound, and we can look at the puppies there," she told me.

I is for
ice cream

Usually, when Momma offers me ice cream I don't ask any questions, but today I had a bunch of them.

"You mean we're not going to see them puppies?" I shouted.

Momma shushed me.

"That's not fair!" I said, and I stomped my foot to the ground to show her I mean business!

"Ellie, you know if you behave that way I will take you home right this minute," Momma told me and she put her hands on her hips, and that's never good.

Oops, I better behave if I want to see them puppies. It's hard sometimes when things don't go my way.

I knew I was being naughty.

"Sorry, Momma," I told her and I threw my arms around her legs to give her a hug.

"Thank you, Ellie. I don't think I thought this through," she said as she rubbed the sides of her head with her fingers.

That must help her think, 'cause she does that a lot.

"You don't have to think nothin' through Momma. You just walk right through those doors, past that store that has the rings and necklaces in the window, and that place where you can make stuffed animals, and there they are waiting for us!" I told her as I tugged on her purse. "They are just right in there!"

"Okay, we'll go in, but no puppies are coming home with us. We are just getting an idea," she told me, as she started walking toward the doors.

Boy was I glad Momma changed her mind 'cause I was getting worried I might miss out on all them puppies!

Puppies must like it to be cold 'cause every time we go over to the mall it's like winter in that place! It's so cold you'd think there were penguins in there and not puppies. I don't care how cold it is in there today 'cause the cold doesn't even bother my excitement!

I could see tails wagging all the way from the stuffed animal store, which made me start running 'cause I couldn't wait to see what was attached to all them happy tails!

Momma was yelling for me to slow down, but I only have one speed when it comes to puppies, and that's full speed fast!

There must have been a lot of other families that had the same idea as us 'cause when we got to the Puppy Play Pen it was real busy.

Maybe they were giving puppies away or something!

"Do you think that's what it is, Momma? Could they be giving them puppies away and that's why it's so crowded?" I asked her.

"It's busy because so many people like to come in and see the puppies, Ellie," she told me.

Momma sure had a big smile on her face. I think she likes them puppies too!

There was a window in front of the store that was as big as the wall!

Inside the window, there were three puppies and two of them puppies were wrestling while another puppy was sleeping in the corner. He must have been super tired 'cause he fell asleep upside down with shredded newspaper all over his face.

"This is the kind I want! I want this kind, please!" I shouted as I pointed to the white, tan, and black puppies.

"Oh no, Ellie, you can't have a dog like that. Those dogs

shed, and your daddy is allergic to dogs that shed. We
have to keep looking," she told me.

"We could keep him in my room so Daddy won't be
allergic," I told her as I watched the puppies play.

"No, that wouldn't be fair to the puppy, honey," Mommy
said.

One of them Puppy Play Pen workers came over to the
window, and she reached in and pulled out one of them
puppies.

The puppy was so happy that he wiggled in her arms and
licked at her face. The worker lady must like puppy kisses

as much as I do 'cause she was laughing as she handed him over to some people.

"Do you think they're buying him, Mommy?" I asked. "I wonder if they are going to take him home?"

"I don't know," Momma said. She grabbed my hand and started walking toward the other windows full of more puppies. "Let's get in the viewing line and see what else they have today."

I couldn't wait to see the rest of them puppies, so I waved goodbye to the white, tan, and black puppies and followed Momma over to the other side of the store.

There were two levels of windows to look through to see all kinds of puppies.

I could see through the bottom windows, but the top

windows were way too high for a little kid like me.

My happy face went to a sad face with this bad news.

"Mommy, I can't see up there. Can you lift me up?" I asked, with my arms raised up high.

When I was smaller, Mommy used to pick me up all the time, so I hope she will today since it's so important and all.

I was happy when she bent over to pick me up! My momma's real strong 'cause she lifted me up and didn't even make a grunting noise like she does when she picks up the water bottles at the store.

There was a Lassie puppy in that top window. I was glad I didn't miss that!

"Oh, that's the dog I want, Momma! It's just like that Lassie dog we saw in all those old Lassie movies we watched at Nannie's!" I told her.

"Sorry kiddo, that's a Collie and it's another dog we can't have. That dog has hair that will make daddy sneeze," Mommy said.

"Can't Daddy just stay in your room?" I asked, but Momma gave me the stink eye again, and I didn't even get to tell her my idea of bringing in his meals on a tray.

"Hmmm, oh my, look at this fella," Momma said as she pointed to a dog that needed a haircut or a hair clip!

"Where are his eyes?" I asked. "Do you think he walks into walls and furniture and stuff, Momma? I bet he does with all that hair hanging in his eyes."

"He looks smart to me, so I bet he gets around just fine," she said.

"Maybe the Puppy Play Pen people will tell his new family that he'll need a hair clip. I bet they will. Maybe we should take him home since we already know that he needs a hair clip," I told her as I started thinking about names for the shaggy pup.

"Oh no, Ellie, that puppy won't be good for Daddy's allergies. See these little guys? This is the type of dog we'll be looking for at the pound," she told me as she pointed at some small dogs that looked like cotton balls with eyes!

There were two white puppies in there, and they were playing with a toy hot dog that was as long as they were!

**H is for hotdog.**

One of them little sweeties had his front paw up and was swatting at that toy hot dog.

"What do you think that puppy is saying to the other puppy, Momma?" I asked.

"Maybe he's saying…'hey, you, puppy, you share that hot dog with me'!" Momma said.

I just love it when Momma does pretend with me.

"Maybe he's wondering when they are going to find a home on account of him being tired of living in this glass box!" I said.

"I'm sure they'll find good homes, Ellie. Don't worry about that," Momma said.

"I think them puppies need a home today, Momma. Why don't we just take one…"

"Ellie, we made a deal. We just came here to look. No puppies today," Momma said without even letting me finish my question!

Even Momma would say that is just *rude*!

"Besides, that particular puppy is expensive and there are so many dogs that need homes. We're not going to shop for a puppy; we're going to adopt a puppy. Don't forget, you still have a week until it's officially your birthday," Mommy said as she put me back down on the ground.

"Excuse me," a man said to my mommy. "I hope you don't mind my interruption, but I overheard you saying that you preferred to adopt a puppy instead of buying one."

"Um, well, yes, that's right," Mommy said.

"Well, the Puppy Play Pen is an adoption boutique," he

said as he handed her a paper. "This explains what we do," he told her.

"What does that mean?" Mommy asked.

"All the puppies here are from rescues or have been rescued from the dog pound. We don't buy from puppy mills or breeders. If you do decide to get a dog from the Puppy Play Pen, you will be adopting a puppy or dog in need," he said.

"We are so lucky, Momma!" I said as I jumped up and down. "We can pick one of them puppies now, since this is one of them adopting places!"

"Thank you for the information. Unfortunately, I've already made other plans, but this is good information to have,"

Mommy told him. "I'll be sure to tell my friends about you."

"Mommy, pleeeeeease! Why can't I have a puppy now?" I asked her, and I gave her my best sad face.

My sad face didn't work. I got a stink eye from her, and that means no.

"We will be waiting, Ellie," she said as she grabbed my hand and headed to leave.

Then Momma messed up my hair, which is what she does when she wants me to agree with her.

"You said I have seven days left until my birthday. Seven whole days left until I turn six," I said, as I waved goodbye to them puppies.

"Don't wish your life away," she told me, but she always tells me that!

I don't know what she means by that, but I'm saving all my wishes for getting that puppy!

## Chapter Three

### Happy Birthday to me!

This week was the longest week of my whole life, but today is finally my birthday!

I'm six today, and I'm never gonna have to wait to be six again!

Momma is making me a special birthday breakfast, and Daddy is putting a box in the car so we can go and get my new puppy!

I don't want to eat, but Momma says I'll need my energy. She's right 'cause I'm gonna play with a puppy later, so I eat real quick-like.

Even though Momma tells me to slow down, I just can't. Just knowing that a puppy is waiting for me is making me want to hurry!

When we got in the van, Daddy gave me the job of holding the collar and the leash, and I'm good at it already! He said it was important to have a collar and a leash for the puppy so that the puppy won't run away. He said it was our respom...respomba...re-spon-si-bil-ity, to keep the puppy safe.

Now I get why I had to wait until I was six 'cause I don't know if I would have been able to handle all of the respom...um, puppy chores when I was five.

The dog place is too far away to count songs, and it looks like a farm to me. There are cows, sheep, horses and a big red barn.

How come every barn I see is red?

I guess all the farmers must like red 'cause I've never seen a purple barn or a blue barn or a yellow barn. I just keep seeing red barns! I have to remember to ask Daddy about it when there isn't so much exciting stuff going on. Daddy knows the answer to just about everything on account of him being an adult smarty.

When we got to the farm, this lady carrying a bucket of apples came out to meet us. She says to call her Kitty, and I like her right away! I like the way she smiles, and she said she was happy we were there.

I tell her I'm happy we're there too, and 'sides, where are them puppies?

Both Mommy and Daddy gave me the stink eye. Kitty just smiled and said to follow her.

I'm excited 'cause Kitty is leading us right to that red barn! I've never been in a barn before, and I can't wait to see inside!

The barn is humungous inside and is also P.U. smelly, but Kitty doesn't seem to mind. She keeps on smiling and is talking to Mommy and Daddy about the weather. I don't know how they can even think about anything but puppies at a time like this!

"Hello there."

We heard a voice but I didn't see where it was coming from.

"Hi Buddy!" Kitty said as she pointed to a daddy who was throwing around big blocks of hay from one part of the barn to another.

Kitty said that he was bringing down more hay for the horses.

He looks like a cowboy to me. I wave at him, and he waves back. He must like working with that hay 'cause he looked real happy.

We walked through the barn, and Kitty took us over to a

stall and opened up the gate.

There's a white momma dog and two puppies in there, and they are just like them puppies we saw at the mall! They were all wiggly and running around all crazy! Kitty ran over and closed the gate so that they wouldn't escape. Neither one of them puppies had a collar, so we had to be real careful and keep them safe.

"Momma, these are just like them puppies from the mall! Do you remember, Momma?" I asked her as I tugged on her shirt.

"How could I forget?" Momma said, which is just crazy 'cause Momma always forgets! Like sometimes when I ask for a hot dog for lunch, and she will tell me "in a minute" well, it's sometimes longer than a minute.

Sometimes, I just have to ask her again 'cause I think she completely forgets! So now I just ask her if it's gonna to be a short minute or a long minute and that way I know if I should get a snack while I'm waitin'.

Kitty says that their doggies were all rescued from a place that didn't take care of them. They were all sick, but Kitty made them all better, and now they are healthy!

Three of them puppies have already been adopted, so there are just two little cuties left, and I get to pick one!

I can't believe how great it is to be six!

Only one problem though...which one should I pick?

They are too cute!

It's like when we go to the ice cream store, and I never can decide if I want Chocolate Chunk or Mint Chocolate Chip. Now, the ice cream place added another one of my favorites, Banana Split Bubble Gum, so I got a whole new set of problems.

"Momma, can we get two puppies so they can stay friends?" I ask.

"You'll be the puppy's friend," Daddy said.

"But...but, Daddy...if we only take home one puppy, that

other puppy will just be lonely," I said, but he was already shaking his head. That's "quiet" for no.

"Why don't you spend a little time playing with the puppies and see which one you like best?" Kitty asked.

Kitty must be a smarty too 'cause that seemed like a real good idea to me.

"Let's take them outside and let them have some room to run around, and maybe that will help you make your decision. Grab a puppy and follow me," she said.

I bent over to pick up a puppy, and he jumped up and licked my nose! He was jumping up so high that I had to check under his furry legs to see if he was on a trampoline or something!

Once I got that little guy in my arms, he just squirmed and licked at my face like he never tasted anything so good!

Kitty told me to put my pup down in the yard, and it seemed like he went to running before he even hit the ground!

When I sat down on the ground, they starting jumping all over me like I had dog food in my pockets! They just jumped on me and ran all around me, then they jumped on me some more!

"What do you think, honey?" Mommy asked me. She had a big smile!

"I think I want to stay here all the time!" I told her as I played with the puppies.

"She can stay there while we fill out the paperwork for the adoption. We'll just be on the other side of that door so we can keep an eye on her," Kitty told Mommy and Daddy.

"Oh, you puppies are so precious! I love you both!" I told them.

Those puppies were all white and fluffy like clouds, except they had black eyes and black noses.

When they nibbled on my fingers, their little teeth were as sharp as pins!

One of them puppies put his head down between his front legs with his bottom sticking straight up to the sky! He

wiggled it and barked at me. When I laughed, he came
charging over and jumped on my lap! I decided right then
that this was the puppy for me!

Wait just a minute!

Just when I thought I picked out my puppy, the other
puppy plopped down in front of me and rolled over and

started barking at me!

Now I didn't know which puppy I wanted.

"How are we doing out here? Did you pick a puppy?" Momma asked me.

"It's hard, Momma. They are both as sweet as can be!" I told her 'cause it was true.

"How do you even tell them apart?" Daddy asked. "They look exactly alike."

"One of the puppies has a tighter curl in his hair, and that's how I tell them apart," Kitty said.

"I still can't tell them apart," Daddy said, 'cause he's not good at dog hair stuff.

Suddenly, one of them puppies came running out from under a bush and was covered with flowers! He had so many flowers on him that he was more flower than puppy!

"Look, Daddy! Now you can tell them apart!" I shouted as I pointed at the puppy.

"Maybe that one is trying to tell us something," Momma said as she wiped the flowers off the puppy.

"Oh, these puppies don't talk, Momma," I told her. I'm surprised Momma didn't know that about puppies, since she's an adult smartie and all.

Maybe she just forgot with all the excitement of picking out a puppy.

"No honey, Mommy means that maybe that puppy has made himself stand out so we'll pick him," Daddy said.

"Oh...well, okay!" I said, and I ran over and picked up that puppy. "Do you want to come home with us, little guy? Do you?"

"That's a fine choice," Kitty said. She bent down and picked up the puppy that we didn't pick.

"Where are you taking him?" I asked, 'cause he had such a sad little puppy face.

"We'll put him back in the stall with his mother until another family comes along that wants to adopt a puppy," Kitty said.

"What happens if no one comes?" I asked.

"Someone will come, don't worry," she said. "Do you want to pet him goodbye?"

I went over to that sweet puppy and kissed his fluffy head.

"Can we please take this puppy too?" I asked. "It makes me so sad to think he'll be all alone."

47

"Someone will come for him, Ellie," Daddy said. "We just came for one puppy, remember?"

Kitty came back without the puppy and told mommy that she was going to get her adoption agreement. We could hear that other puppy crying from the barn.

"Is that the puppy crying?" Momma asked Kitty.

"He'll be okay," Kitty said. "He'll miss his brother for a couple of days and then he'll adjust. I'll be calling you folks in a few days to check on how things are going, and I'll give you an update on how he's doing. Now, you've got a lot of responsibility that comes with that puppy, Ellie. Do you understand?"

"Oh yes! I'm ready!" I told her, 'cause I totally meant it! I was ready to be that puppy's best friend.

"We'll only let you take the puppy home if you promise to

take care of it. Are you going to feed him?" Kitty asked.

"I will feed him every day!" I told her. "Plus, I'll give him dog treats when he does the tricks I'm going to teach him!"

"What about fresh water? He'll need fresh water every day. That's important," Kitty said.

"We bought him a new food bowl and new water bowl yesterday, and I'll be sure he has fresh water. I promise," I told her.

"He'll need you to be very gentle with him. You don't want to drop him, or tug at his tail or ears. Puppies like it when you pet them softly and give them gentle hugs. They want a family that loves them. Can you do that?" Kitty asked as we walked out to our van.

"That's easy! He's already in my heart 'cause I already love him!" I told her as I gave him a gentle hug.

H is for heart.

"You have to walk him, play with him, and protect him," Kitty said. "Whatever rules your parents set for your new puppy, you have to teach him. A puppy likes it when he knows the rules. He wants to be a member of the family too," Kitty said. "Ellie, a puppy isn't a friend for just a little while. He won't always be a cuddly puppy. When you adopt a puppy, it means that you promise to love him and take care of him for his whole life, no matter what. Do you understand?"

I looked at Mommy and Daddy, and they nodded their heads and smiled. I guess there was a lot more to getting a puppy 'sides just picking out a new water bowl and collar.

"I'm ready," I told Kitty. "I'll take good care of your puppy."

Ss

S is for squirrel.

"He's your puppy now," she told me and she gave me a hug before I got in the van and put the puppy in his box.

Then she gave us a stuffed squirrel that had been in the stall with the puppies and their mommy. She said it will smell like his mommy, and to put it in bed with the puppy to help him sleep.

"Call if you need anything!" Kitty yelled as Daddy pulled away from the farm.

"Is that lady crazy?" I asked. "What else could we need? We just got a new puppy!"

# Chapter Four

## Puppy Misses Mommy

The very first thing that puppy did when we got to our house was go right in and make a big ol' mess.

He must not like newspapers, 'cause Mommy and Daddy put newspapers all over the floor, but he found a spot they missed.

Momma must be trying to think of something 'cause she's rubbing the sides of her head again.

"Ellie, take the puppy right outside, and put him down where we decided he will be going potty," Momma told me.

I picked up that puppy, ran outside with him, and set him down in the corner by the fence. He looked at me and sat down on his furry little bottom.

"Why you're so cute I think I'll have to name you Cutie," I told him. He seemed to think that was okay 'cause he got up and wagged his tail at me.

We ran inside so I could tell everyone what I decided to name him.

"Guess what, guys!" I yelled when I came in the house. "I'm going to call this puppy Cutie on account of him being so cute!"

Daddy came over with a pad of paper and a pen.

"Ellie, that's a good choice and I'm going to put it on this sheet of paper. I would like you to keep thinking of names for your puppy, and then tomorrow morning when you get up, you can decide which of the names on the list you like best," Daddy said.

That seemed like a brainy idea to me 'cause I was already thinking of other names for that puppy.

Daddy is smart, and that's why he takes the train to an office every day for work, and you have to be smart to work at an office.

When I grow up, I want to work at a store and be a cashier. I like playing "shop" with Mommy and pretending to be a cashier. Real cashiers get to play with real money, and that seems like a good job for me!

Momma says that I should keep my options open, but I don't even know where I put my options.

Maybe I could be a dog walker 'cause then I could bring my dog with me, or maybe I could work at the Puppy Play Pen. I know, I could be a cashier at the Puppy Play Pen!

I gotta remember that for when I get a job when I'm older, 'cause that sounds real good to me!

"Okay, Daddy, that list idea seems like a real smarty idea. I really like Cutie, but it's good to have a list, just in case. I like Marshmella too, 'cause he does look like a marshmella. Why don't you put that on the list too, Daddy?" I asked him.

"Can we make suggestions for your list?" Momma asked. She came over to pet that puppy, and she seemed to

forget that he made that big ol' mess, 'cause she was letting that puppy lick her face.

"Sure!" I told her, 'cause Momma always has good ideas. "We can all put names on the list, but I want to pick the final name! Can I, Momma? Can I be the one that gets to pick the puppy's name?"

"Yes, honey, you can pick the name. You have the rest of tonight, and you don't have to decide anything until tomorrow morning. Right now, we have to get the puppy used to his crate, because soon the two of you will need to get ready for bed," she said.

"How about Murphy?" Daddy says. "I used to have a dog named Murphy."

"Put it on the list," Mommy said, as she moved the crate. "Let's add Scooby too."

"Scooby? Okay, what about Duke?" Daddy asked as he wrote the names down on the list.

"You gotta add Cotton and Cloud please, Daddy!" I yelled 'cause picking out a puppy name was exciting!

Momma gave me a blanket to put in the puppy's crate.

The crate is big enough for me to sit in, but Momma says I can't go in there. She said the crate is just for the puppy, so he has his very own place in the house.

Maybe for my next birthday I'll ask them for a crate of my very own!

"Kitty said we should put a wind-up clock in the crate with the puppy. She says the ticking will help him sleep and not miss his mother and siblings so much," Daddy said.

"What's a sibling?" I asked as I looked over the list of

names.

"The puppy's brothers and sisters," Momma answered. "This will be his first night without his family."

"Oh, the poor puppy!" I cried. "We took that sweet puppy away from his momma and his brother! He must be so sad being away from them."

"We're his new family, Ellie," Daddy told me. "It's normal for a puppy to separate from his family. We'll just help him through the first couple of nights. Don't forget we have the stuffed squirrel that Kitty gave us to comfort him, but he'll adjust quickly."

Even though Daddy said it would be okay, I still felt sad for that little puppy.

"I think that he should have a friend his first night. Can I sleep with him?" I asked them, as I crossed my fingers for them to say yes.

Mommy nodded her head, which means yes!

"Please get the alarm clock from your room, Ellie and wind it up and put it in the cage with the puppy. You can put your sleeping bag down in front of his cage so he can see you. Maybe that will help him sleep," Momma said.

After Mommy and Daddy went to bed, I was in charge of that little puppy.

He whined and cried, and it about broke my heart into a million cazillion pieces.

I stuck my fingers through the holes in the crate, and he came over and licked them before he finally decided to go to sleep.

He rested his fluffy head on that stuffed squirrel and got comfy. It took a real long time, but I think all that whining finally just wore that little puppy out.

When he couldn't cry anymore, he just finally fell asleep.

The clock I put in the cage had the little hand on the one and the big hand on the twelve.

I couldn't tell what time it was, but I think it was late o'clock!

Last year, Mommy and Daddy let me stay up for New Year's Eve.

That's when the old year changes into a new year, and that was the latest I ever got to stay up, but tonight I think it's even later.

I couldn't wait until morning, so I could tell Mommy and Daddy that I got that sweet puppy to sleep, but then the worst thing that could ever happen happened!

That dumb ol' alarm clock went off!

"Riiiing! Riiiing! Riiiing! Riiiing!"

It rang so loud that the puppy jumped up and started crying like somebody stepped on his tail or something!

Mommy and Daddy both ran out into the family room while I tried to get the crate open.

"Ellie! What happened?" Mommy asked, as she came over and opened up the crate.

"I guess the alarm clock went off," I told her, quiet-like.

"I guess," Momma said, all tired-like as she ruffled my hair.

Momma kissed me goodnight, took the alarm clock and went back to bed with Daddy.

That puppy just looked at me and started up with his cryin' again.

I bet this must be the respomb...responnsa, responsibility that Kitty was talking about back at the barn.

# Chapter Five

## Time to name that puppy!

When I got up this morning, I was excited 'cause today was the day we were gonna name that puppy!

Daddy said there were fourteen names to choose from on the list.

Dog names:

Cutie, Mister Whister, Cotton, Wheezie, Murphy, Snickerdoodle, Cloud, Buster, Duke, Scoobie, Marshmella, Skippy, Kirby, Winston

"This is hard, Daddy," I said. "I want to make sure that I give him the perfect name, 'cause he's going to have it for almost his whole life."

"Well, he will have it for his whole life," Daddy said as he poured me some juice.

"No, that's not right, Daddy," I said. "Kitty said that he is twelve weeks old, so that is twelve weeks of his life that he didn't have no name."

"Any name," Daddy said.

"Huh?" I asked him.

"You said that he didn't have *no* name, but what you should have said was that he didn't have *any* name," Daddy told me.

He's always fixing the way I talk 'cause he wants me to be a smarty too.

"I'm sure you'll make the right decision," Momma said as she drank her juice.

"Who named me?" I asked.

"We did," Daddy said.

"How did you decide to call me Ellie?" I asked.

"We named you after your mommy's mommy because she is a special woman," Daddy said.

"But her name is Grandma!" I said, 'cause this was getting confusing.

"Well, true, you call her Grandma, but her given name is Eleanor, or Ellie for short," Momma said. "We like to call you Ellie."

My whole life I thought I had just a regular ol' name, but now I know that I have the same name as Grandma Ellie! I think that's super neat since she's so sweet and all.

"So do you think I should name that puppy after someone I love?" I asked them.

"That's the great thing about naming a puppy, Elle," Daddy said.

He calls me Elle when Ellie is just too much to say.

"You can name him anything you want, Elle. He'll be happy with whatever name you choose because he knows you love him. Just go with what makes you happy, honey," Daddy told me as he tapped the list with his pencil.

I looked at that list a few more times and decided to name that puppy Skippy Marshmella Carmichael!

"Are you sure?" Daddy asked. "That's a lot of names for such a little dog."

"Yes, Daddy, I'm sure," I told him. "I like the name Skippy, and he looks like a marshmella, and our last name is Carmichael, which means his last name would be Carmichael."

"Yes, dear, but dogs don't typically have three names," Momma explained.

"But if he only had one name, what would I call him when he's naughty?" I asked.

Momma didn't answer, but her whole face got real red.

I don't know how Momma does that, but she can change the color of her face, real quick-like! One minute it's normal color, and then it's bright red!

SKIPPY MARSHMELLA
CARMICHAEL

I hope I get to learn how to do that.

"Okay, so Skippy Marshmella it is," Daddy said, putting his list away 'cause we wouldn't be using it anymore.

"Skippy Marshmella Carmichael, Daddy," I said 'cause he needed reminding.

"Right, got it, dear," he said, correcting his list.

"Don't forget, Ellie, Skippy will need to go outside every hour so he can get used to where he will be going potty. You have to watch him all the time to make sure he's not chewing on anything that he's not supposed to be chewing on, which means, anything that is not a chew toy. Can you remember that?" Momma asked, as she wiped her hands on a dish towel.

Well, that's a silly question 'cause it was only two things to remember, and I have to remember lots and lots more

than that when I'm at school every day! I have to remember how to count and to keep my hands to myself, so that's already two things to remember. I get to be Teacher's Helper every Monday, and she gives me lots to remember like turning off the lights, and collecting all the crayons when we do crafts.

I just know I'll be able to remember the stuff Mommy wants me to remember.

"No problemo," I told Mommy except she wasn't smiling. She had her serious face on, and I'm sure there was a stink eye comin'.

"Would you like to take Skippy over to the park this morning and let him run around?" Daddy asked.

"Yay! I would love to go to the park!" I yelled, and gave Daddy a big hug.

I like going to the park 'cause all my friends play at the park!

It would be so neat if maybe they would be there, and then they could meet Skippy!

"Daddy, will you watch Skippy for me so I can go get my weekend clothes on?" I asked.

Weekend clothes are shirts that aren't red, white, or blue. I gotta wear those colors to school, so I never wear red, white or blue shirts on the weekend. This way my school clothes can get a break.

Daddy said he'd watch Skippy, so I ran into my room, got my weekend clothes on, and ran right back out to that

puppy.

"Let's go, Daddy, let's go!" I shouted as I pulled on his arm.

"Hold your horses, Ellie," Daddy said as he twirled me around and gave me a kiss.

"What horses are you talking about, Daddy?" I asked him, looking around. "Momma would never let us have horses in the kitchen."

Daddy laughed and told me that it just means that I should slow down. If he wanted me to slow down, why didn't he just say slow down? Why bring horses into the whole thing anyway?

"Ellie, finish your breakfast, and we'll go after we're done eating," he told me.

We had pancakes for breakfast. I gobbled it up quick-like 'cause I knew that when I was done we were going to the park, and I really wanted to get this puppy to the park!

"No, no, nooooooo!" Momma yelled as she ran into the room.

Daddy and I were too busy with our breakfast to notice that Skippy had decided to chew on something 'sides his chew toy, and that something belonged to Momma.

It was her shoe.

"Ellie, you are responsible for watching your puppy, and now look what he's done to my shoe," she said as she held it out. "See how this shoe is all shiny and new? Now notice how this shoe has teeth marks all over it? Well, this is ruined. I'll never be able to wear them again."

"I'm sorry, Momma," I told her, with a frowny on my face. I felt bad that Skippy ruined her shoe.

"Just don't let him out of your sight!" Momma said as she turned and walked into her room. Daddy got up from the table and followed her.

That's when I got a real brainy idea! Momma said that her shoes were ruined 'cause Skippy chewed on *one* of them. Well, I can't fix the shoe that Skippy chewed on, but I can sure change the shiny and new one!

"Come here, Skippy!" I called at that puppy, but he didn't come since we just decided his name, and no one even told him.

Yeah, we must have forgot.

"Hey, puppy! Your name is Skippy Marshmella Carmichael! Come on Skippy, come here, boy!" I said.

I went and got that puppy 'cause he still wasn't used to his name yet, and I gave him Mommy's shiny new shoe. I didn't even have to tell him what to do!

He got that shoe in his mouth and went right to chewing on it! Wow, he was doing a real good job too!

"Ellie Maureen Carmichael!" Mommy yelled. "What on earth are you doing?"

I jumped up 'cause she didn't sound happy, but I knew when Skippy was finished she was going to be very happy! I quickly grabbed that shoe from Skippy and held it out for Momma to see.

"Here you go, Momma! Now you have two shoes that are

exactly the same, and you can wear them again 'cause they match!" I told her.

I was real proud that I fixed the shoes, Skippy helped, but it was my brainy idea.

Momma must have been in complete happy shock, 'cause she didn't say anything.

"Richie, can you come in here, please!" Momma shouted to Daddy.

Richie is what Mommy calls Daddy when she talks parent.

"What is it?" Daddy asked her when he walked in the room.

Mommy handed Daddy her shoes and told him that she needed a time-out.

I don't understand why she needed a time-out 'cause she didn't break any house rules, but Daddy must have seen something I didn't 'cause he told her that he understood.

I wonder how long Mommy will have to be in time-out? When I get a time-out, I have to do one minute for every year of how old I am so now that I just turned six, I get six minutes in time-out.

Wow...Momma's gonna be in time-out for a long time!

# Chapter Six

## Skippy Meets Whisper

I'm so excited 'cause Daddy says it's time to take Skippy to the park!

I ran to get Skippy's brand spankin' new leash that matched his purple collar.

The first thing that little guy did was put that leash in his mouth and give it a good chew.

"No, no chew, little Skippy," I told him, soft like since he's new and all.

I decided that maybe I should wait and try out the whole leash thing when we get outside.

Boy does he love it outside!

When I opened the door, he ran outside to the porch. He

pranced and jumped around until he wandered too close to the step and fell off! That puppy bounced off the step, tumbled down to the next step, and then landed in a furry ball on the sidewalk!

"Oh no!" I yelled, 'cause I was scared he got hurt. "Are you okay, Skippy? You okay, fella?"

That puppy must have been fine 'cause he was up and wrestlin' with that leash like it was a chew toy or something.

"Ellie, don't let Skippy chew on his leash. We don't want him to think it's a toy," Daddy said, as he came down the steps.

Daddy should know 'cause when he was little he had a dog, so he's a kind of dog expert, like the guy that we watch on television, the Dog Whimperer.

I reached down and pulled the leash out of Skippy's mouth. He barked at me, real playful like, and then grabbed that leash and tugged at it again!

"No!" I yelled, but he was having too much fun playing to listen.

"Hold the leash straight up over Skippy's head so he can't get it in his mouth, Ellie," Daddy told me.

So I listened to Daddy and did exactly what he told me to do, and that silly ol' dog decided just to flip over on his back and try to swat at the leash with his little legs.

Then out of nowhere came that sneaky cat from next door, Whisper.

He was always running around the yard and jumping out of the bushes to scare us!

Skippy stopped playing with the leash and pranced right on over to Whisper like they were buddies or something, but Whisper didn't want anything to do with that new puppy. He made a loud cat noise and slapped at Skippy with his orange cat paw before running away.

Poor, little Skippy turned around and yelped! He ran past me, and tried to run up the stairs, but he's just too little to escape that way, so he ran back to me.

Daddy bent down and picked up Skippy. That little Skippy was still whimpering.

"He's shaking like he's cold or something," I said, and I was worried for that little guy.

"Well, now he knows to stay away from Whisper," Daddy said. "Let's get him to the park."

"The park? Oh YEAH!" I said 'cause I completely forgot about the park!

I guess my puppy being attacked by the neighbor's cat made me forget that the whole time we were on the way to the park!

I carried Skippy just in case Whisper decided to come back and scare him again.

Maybe Whisper will let Skippy be his friend one day, but I don't think today is the day!

When we got to the park, I could see that MiShaun May was there with her mother and our friend from school, Landon.

I like MiShaun and all, but she's just not the nicest person in my class.

Momma says to be nice to everyone, including MiShaun,

but there is just something about that girl that makes it hard.

She calls me Ellie So Smelly, but I'm not smelly, and I know she knows that's not my name. The teacher says my real name every morning when she takes attendance, and MiShaun sits right up front, so I know she hears her, but she still calls me Ellie So Smelly!

There's another girl in class named Joanie Maloney, but MiShaun calls her Joanie Bolognie just to be a meanie. Joanie said the name calling hurt her feelings so much that she can't eat bolognie no more!

MiShaun does naughty real good, but Mommy says to be nice, so I'm nice, but it's hard to be that good.

"Ellie So Smelly, what have you got!" MiShaun yelled from her picnic table for the whole world to hear.

She was having a sandwich with Landon. I bet she eats bolognie with no problem.

"My name is Ellie Carmichael, MiShaun, and this here is my brand spankin' new puppy, Skippy!" I said.

"Skippy?" MiShaun asked, like she can't believe it and all. "Like the peanut butter? You named your dog after peanut butter?"

Oh no, I gotta be careful 'cause she's bringing up peanut butter!

"No, I named him Skippy 'cause he skips around all the time 'cause he's so happy that he's a puppy and all," I said. Whew!

I thought of that real quick-like.

I don't want her to ruin peanut butter for me like she ruined bolognie for Joanie. I just couldn't imagine my life without peanut butter and jelly sandwiches!

"It's a silly name, but can I hold him?" she asked, and I wanted to say no, 'cause of her calling me names and all, but Daddy already told her yes. He was taking Skippy out of my arms and putting him down on the ground like it's *his* dog or something.

"He's such a sweet puppy," Landon said.

"Oh, he's as cute as he can be, Ellie!" she said as Skippy jumped all over her and covered her with puppy kisses. "You have to be the luckiest girl I know to have this sweet, adorable puppy all to yourself, Ellie!"

Now I know that it's an exciting time, with the new puppy

and all, but I just couldn't believe what my ears were hearing!

Two times MiShaun used my name, and neither time did she add "So Smelly" to it!

Having a puppy is the coolest thing ever! Maybe she

won't wanna be mean anymore, and we can be friends!

"He's giving me kisses!" Landon said, as he rolled in the grass and giggled.

"Can I walk him, Ellie?" MiShaun asked, but she was already walking away with him before I even said she could!

"Be careful with him on account of him being new and all," I told her.

"What do you think I'm going to do, break him?" she said, all "MiShaun-like."

"This is the first time he's ever been on a leash, so he's new to it," Daddy told her.

"Don't worry, I've walked dogs before," MiShaun told him as she walked away with Skippy and Landon beside her.

Just then, that little Skippy crossed over in front of MiShaun, and she tripped over his leash, fell to the ground and landed right on her face!

"Oh no!" Landon yelled. "Puppy took MiShaun down!"

"It's not funny, Landon," MiShaun said as she wiped her mouth.

"Are you okay?" I asked as she was getting up, 'cause she was making this weird moaning noise that sounded like the black bears we saw on the Wildlife channel last weekend.

"I'm bleeding!" she screamed and her momma and my daddy came running over. "That puppy tripped me!"

"Well, he did say that the puppy never walked with a leash before," Landon said.

"Be quiet, Landon!" MiShaun yelled. "He tripped me on

80

purpose!"

"Don't be silly, MiShaun," her mother told her. "He's just a little puppy. It was an accident."

Skippy must not have felt too bad, 'cause he was busy chewing on that purple leash again.

"Oh my, looks like you lost a tooth," Daddy said.

"Cha-Ching! That's money, MiShaun!" Landon yelled as he raised his hand for MiShaun to give him a high five.

MiShaun didn't want to give him a high five.

"A tooth? MOMMY! MY TOOTH IS MISSING!" MiShaun yelled. She was crying, and her mommy was holding a napkin up to her mouth.

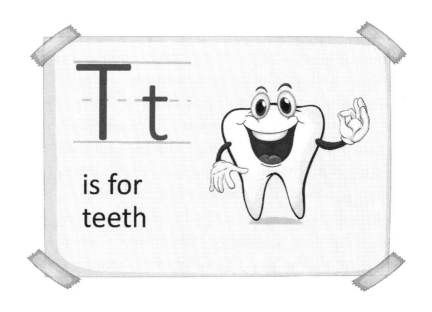

T t

is for
teeth

"This is all your puppy's fault, Ellie So Smelly!"

"I'm so sorry about the lost tooth," Daddy said to

MiShaun's mommy. "Is there anything we can do?"

"Teach that puppy some manners!" MiShaun said as she
sobbed into her napkin.

"Girls…," Landon muttered as he rolled his eyes.

"Landon, this is very serious! Please stop it!" MiShaun
said between sobs.

"Sorry," Landon said, as he turned toward the street. "I'm
going home. Good luck with the Tooth Fairy!"

"Be careful, Landon. Stay on the sidewalk!" MiShaun's
mom yelled to Landon.

"Got it!" he yelled back.

"Ah, hellooooooo!" MiShaun said as she pointed to her mouth. "I'm dying here, remember?"

"I think you'll survive this," MiShaun's mom told her. She said that MiShaun's tooth was already loose, and that they were waiting for it to fall out. She said it would be great if we could help find it so MiShaun could put it under her pillow for the Tooth Fairy.

So we searched the grass for MiShaun's dumb ol' tooth, but we never could find it.

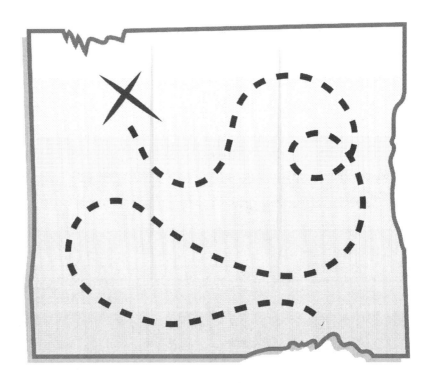

Poor MiShaun was gonna have to write a note for the Tooth Fairy to tell her the tooth is somewhere in the park.

I told MiShaun that the Tooth Fairy probably had something kind of like a metal detector, except for teeth.

A tooth detector, I guess.

"Maybe you could draw the Tooth Fairy a map of where we were, and she'll be able to find it with her tooth detector," I told her.

"A tooth detector isn't real, Ellie So Smelly," MiShaun said. "You don't know anything!"

MiShaun's mom said that MiShaun wasn't the first girl to loose her tooth in a park. She also said that MiShaun should say she is sorry to me 'cause I was just trying to help, but MiShaun didn't, and she seemed sad when she started walking back to their house.

"I'm sorry, Daddy," I said, as I hugged him.

"It was an accident so there is no need to worry," Daddy told me.

Even though MiShaun could be mean with her words, I still felt bad that she was so sad.

I bent down to pet Skippy and I felt a little, white rock fall off his back. I wondered where he could have gotten a rock since there weren't any rocks around us.

Wait a minute!

That's not a little, white rock!

I couldn't believe my little eyes! Right there in his curly fur was MiShaun's tooth!

"Daddy, look at this!" I yelled, 'cause I was so excited. "It's MiShaun's tooth!"

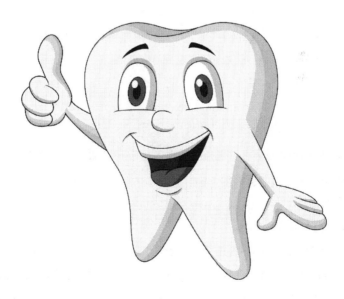

# Ss

S is for school.

"Well, isn't that lucky! Pick up Skippy and let's run and see if we can catch up with MiShaun. She'll be so happy that you found the tooth!" Daddy said, and he smiled a humongous smile!

I picked up Skippy, and we ran real fast and caught up with MiShaun. She was still crying.

"Dry your eyes, kid," I told her as I held up the tooth for her to see. "You'll be able to stick your tooth under your pillow, after all!"

"You found it? Thank you so much, Ellie," she said, as she hugged her mother. She smiled at me, and I could see where that tooth had once been 'cause now she had a big ol' hole right in front.

"That's okay. You know, if you wanted to you could stick a straw through where your tooth used to be, and you wouldn't have to open your mouth to drink now!" I told her, 'cause it wouldn't be right to keep that kind of cool information to myself.

She liked that idea and was all smiley when she left with her mommy.

"I'll see you at school," I told her, as she walked away.

Maybe MiShaun isn't as bad as I thought.

"Okay, see you at school, Ellie So Smelly," she answered.

Shows you what I know.

"Good boy, Skippy," I said as I kissed that sweet dog. "You made her very happy even if she is a meanie."

"Ellie, please be nice," Daddy said, as we started walking home.

Well, meanie or not, I'm glad that MiShaun got her tooth back.

I have a feeling that Skippy is going to make a lot of people happy!

## Chapter Seven

### Skippy gets a playmate!

When we got back from the park, I couldn't wait to tell Momma what happened to MiShaun and her tooth! Mommy was waiting for us on our porch.

"Momma! MiShaun was at the park, and she got to meet Skippy, and when she was walking him, she tripped over his leash and fell, and her tooth fell out, and she cried 'cause we couldn't find it, and then she started to go home and then, guess what?" I asked her, out of breath.

"What honey?" Mommy asked me as she laughed.

"I found her tooth in Skippy's fur and we ran after them so we could give it back to her. She was so happy we found her tooth, 'cause now she can put it under her pillow for the Tooth Fairy! But guess what?" I asked her.

"What dear?" Mommy asked.

"I found her tooth and all, but she still called me Ellie So Smelly!" I told her.

"What did I tell you about that?" Mommy asked me.

"That it's her problem and not mine," I told her.

"Exactly, you be nice, and you'll get nice back, but if she doesn't stop we'll talk to the teacher. Now, please take Skippy outside and see if he has to go potty while I talk to Daddy. Please hurry!" Mommy said.

We just got back from being outside, but I took Skippy to his little corner of the yard anyway.

He didn't mind 'cause he loves to be outside!

We had only been outside for a couple of minutes before Mommy called for us to come back in the house.

When we came back in, Mommy looked super happy, and Daddy looked like he does when he doesn't feel well.

"Ellie, we have a surprise for you. I think it's wonderful, but Daddy is still getting used to the idea. Anyway, Kitty called to check to see how things were going with Skippy, and she mentioned that the other little puppy still had not found a home. She also said that he seemed very sad. He cries a lot, and she's worried about him," Mommy said.

"That's sad!" I told her. "We need to go back and get him, Momma!"

"Well, that's the surprise, Ellie," Mommy said and she gave me a humungous smile!

"Does that mean...," I started to ask, but the words wouldn't come out of my mouth on account of my mouth not believing what I was trying to say!

"It means we're going back to get the other puppy, right now!" Mommy said.

"We ARE?" I screamed as I jumped up and down in the kitchen. "YA-HOO!"

Skippy must have understood because he was barking and jumping up and down!

"I can't believe it, Momma!" I said. "Thank you, thank you, thank you! I just can't believe we are going to have another puppy! This is the neatest thing that has ever happened to me in my whole life!"

"It is very exciting," Mommy said. "We have to leave now, so we can make it there and back before it gets too late."

"Are you okay, Daddy?" I asked, 'cause Daddy still didn't look too good.

"He'll be okay, honey," Mommy said. "You will be okay, won't you, Richie? Maybe I should drive."

When we got back to the barn, Kitty was waiting for us with the other puppy!

Daddy let Skippy out of the van, and the brothers ran to each other and started wrestling on the grass! They were so happy to see each other!

I think Daddy got used to the idea of having two puppies 'cause he had a big smile on his face!

Kitty had some papers for my mommy and daddy to sign, and then we got to take that puppy and put him in our van. I

guess he must have been nervous, 'cause when he got in
he piddled a little on the seat!

"Oh no!" Daddy yelled and he picked the new puppy up
and put him back on the grass.

"That will come out with a little vinegar and baking soda,"
Kitty told him. "You know what, hold on a second."

She ran into that red barn and came back out a minute
later with a bag.

"These are piddle pads. You might need them for this
one," she told Daddy. "Thank you, for providing a home for
these little guys. They'll be so happy being together."

"We're so happy that they are together!" I told her. "Wait!
What about the momma dog? Now she's all alone!"

"Oh boy," Daddy said, and he put his hand up to his head.

He does that when he gets a headache.

"Don't worry, Mr. Carmichael," Kitty said. "The mother dog has already been adopted. She is the newest member of my family, and will join us in the main house to enjoy her days being spoiled."

"Thank goodness," Daddy said. "I'm glad to hear she will be taken care of."

"Yay!" I shouted, 'cause I was excited for her. "Everybody gets a family!"

MiShaun might be a stinker sometimes, but she was right about one thing.

I am the luckiest girl in the whole world!

I'm over the moon!

Well, I'm not really over the moon, but Mommy said that when someone says they are "over the moon" it means they are super duper happy!

So I'm over the moon with super duper happiness!

# Chapter Eight

## Puppies' First Swim!

The whole way home we talked about a name for that new puppy. We still had all the names that we didn't use for Skippy, and I let Mommy and Daddy pick this puppy's name since I got to pick the name for the first puppy.

"You can pick the name this time," I told them, but I got nervous that they'd pick a name I didn't like.

"What about Snickerdoodle?" Mommy said. "I think it sounds sweet with Skippy, and you can call him Snicker for short."

"That's a great name!" I shouted since I was excited. "What about the middle name?"

"What do you think, Richie?" Mommy asked.

95

"Well, let's see...Skippy's middle name is Marshmella, right?" Daddy said. "How about if we go with Cotton Candy, and call him Snickerdoodle Cotton Candy Carmichael?"

"Wow, that's a mouthful!" Mommy said, and then she started laughing.

"I bet it would be a yummy mouthful too, Mommy! Snickerdoodle is a kind of cookie, right?" I asked.

SNICKERDOODLE COTTON CANDY CARMICHAEL

"That's right," she said.

"I bet they are the tastiest cookie and, well, everyone knows how great cotton candy is, so it would be a yummy mouthful for sure!" I said.

With all this talk about cookies and cotton candy my stomach started to growl!

"So, everyone in agreement?" Daddy asked.

"Yep, and do you know what's cool about this name,

Daddy?" I asked.

"What's cool about this name, honey?" Daddy replied.

"It's 'cause Snickerdoodle is just so much fun to say! I could say it all day long! Snickerdoodle, Snickerdoodle, Snickerdoodle!" I told him.

"Well, good! It looks like Mommy picked out a good name then," Daddy said.

So I thought that if I had fun saying Snickerdoodle, then maybe the puppy would have fun listening to it! Snickerdoodle Cotton Candy Carmichael it is!

"Your name is Snickerdoodle, little guy," I told him, so he'd know. "We've been calling your brother Skippy. He seems to like it just fine, so I hope you like your name too!" That puppy licked my whole hand and didn't stop for a super long time, so I think he likes the name.

He either likes the name or he was licking off the juice that I spilled on my hand earlier...no, I think he just really likes the name.

When we got home, we took both puppies through our gate and into the backyard so Snickerdoodle wouldn't make a big ol' mess in the house.

The puppies loved the backyard right away! I can understand why they like it, 'cause I like it too! It's no wonder, on account of us having the coolest backyard ever. We have a fenced in yard, so we can run around all we want! We also have a big ol' tree that my daddy said he'd build a tree house in one day, and, the best part of all, we have a big ol' pool in our backyard too!

I like to go swimming, and I swim in it all the time. It's

probably 'cause I'm part fish...well, that's what my Grandpa
says.

I'm not really part fish, but he likes to say I am, so I don't
mind.

I think it'd be cool to be a fish!

Well, except I don't think I'd like the food much, 'cause

**F f**

is for
fish

it doesn't even look like food.

It looks like crumbs.

Plus, if I was a fish, I just know that I'd miss ice cream,

and cookies,

and cotton candy,

and going to play at the park,

and playing with puppies,

and going to Nannie and Poppie's,

and just everything!

Gosh, I sure am glad I'm not a fish!

"Now that we have two puppies we're going to have to have eyes in the back of our heads," Mommy said.

"That's crazy, Mommy!" I said. "I've never seen anyone with eyes in the back of their head!"

"Mommy just means that we're going to have to keep a close eye on the puppies so they don't get into any trouble," Daddy said.

It's that parent secret language again, I think.

The puppies are so happy to be together again!

They sure love playing, and it seems like their favoritest game of all is Tag. One puppy starts by chasing the other puppy, and then they turn around and switch and the puppy that was doing the chasin' becomes the puppy being chased! The whole time there's a lot of barking going on, and we just watch and try to figure out which puppy is which!

It's all very confusing since they're twins.

Good thing for different color collars.

Whoever had that smarty idea must have had twin puppies!

"Do you think they're playing Tag, Mommy?" I asked as I watched them chase each other around the backyard.

"It sure looks like it, doesn't it," Mommy answered.

Just then, Skippy started running, but instead of looking where he was going, he was looking back at Snickerdoodle and didn't notice he was running right toward the pool!

We all yelled for him to stop, but he doesn't know all the words yet so he didn't understand us, and just kept on with his running.

Skippy ran right into the pool, and Snickerdoodle went in right after him! It sounded like someone threw two rocks in the pool.

Splash! Splash!

"Oh no! Get 'em, get 'em, get 'em!" Mommy yelled, and then she jumped right into that pool at the same time

Daddy did!

I stood there for a second and then I jumped right in with them 'cause I never pass up a chance to go swimming.

"It's coooooooold!" I shouted 'cause I didn't know it was going to be that cold!

We don't usually go swimming when we have to start wearing our jackets at night, and now I sure know why!

Mommy and Daddy scooped up those cold, wet puppies and got out of the pool.

"Ellie, what are you doing in the pool?" Mommy asked as she motioned for me to get out.

She was holding Skippy, and he was licking her face.

That must be how puppies thank you when you save their lives.

"Well, everybody else was in the pool, and you know how you're always telling me I should just go with the flow, Mommy? Well, that's what I was doing. I was going with the flow," I told her. "You know what, Momma?"

"What, honey?" she asked.

"Going with the flow is cold!" I told her.

"Let's get you and the puppies in the house. We'll get some towels to dry off. I don't want anyone getting sick," Momma said.

"You mean we're not going swimming?" I asked as I shook from the cold.

"No honey, we were just afraid that the puppies wouldn't know what to do, so that's why we jumped in," Momma said as she walked over to the sliding door.

"But Daddy said that puppies just know how to swim without even having to take lessons," I said as I followed her.

"Yes, that's true," Daddy said. "It's called instinct, honey."

"Well, if the puppies will just swim on their own, then why did we all jump in after them?" I asked.

"Good question, honey!" Mommy laughed.

Daddy was laughing too.

"When you're a parent, even when you know your child, or puppy, will be okay, you jump in to help anyway, at least when they are little," Mommy said.

"Mommy is right," Daddy told her. "And now you know

that puppies can get into trouble, so we have to watch them closely."

"We need to get warmed up. I'll get the towels and our robes. You guys get out of those wet clothes," Momma said as she handed me Skippy.

Her shoes made a squishy noise when she walked since they weren't used to being worn in the pool.

"I'll start the hot chocolate!" Daddy said as he handed me Snickerdoodle.

He put the blanket that Mommy keeps on the couch around my shoulders while I held the puppies. They seemed to love that they got to go swimming!

"I think they liked the pool, Daddy!" I said as they wiggled in my arms.

"I think they did too, honey," he said, as he started making the hot chocolate.

Mommy came downstairs with robes and towels for all of us, and then she suggested that we order a pizza.

Pizza too?

First we got another brand spankin' new puppy, then we got to jump in the pool with all of our clothes on, and now we're having hot chocolate and ordering a pizza!

I think that being six is gonna be my favoritest age ever!

P is for Pizza

# Chapter Nine

## Daddy Has Big News!

Today at school, my teacher let me get up in front of the whole class and tell them about my little puppies, and it wasn't even Show-n-Tell day!

I got to tell them how we adopted them from a farm with a red barn.

She let me tell the story of them running into our pool, and how me and Mommy and Daddy jumped in to save them!

Plus, I got to tell them that's how come I have this cold now.

I told them it was worth getting the cold though, 'cause it was so much fun jumping in the pool with all my clothes on!

I also told them about how Skippy made a big ol' mess in the house.

The whole class laughed except for Mrs. Norris, but she doesn't ever laugh about nothin'. I think she might be missing her funny bone.

She let me show them pictures that Daddy took of them puppies.

There were some of Skippy at the park and some of both of them puppies in their crate and riding in the van.

After hearing all the fun stuff about the puppies, all the kids from my class wanted to come over to our house to play with them.

Momma has a rule that I have to ask before I have friends over.

Well, we didn't have any "before" time, since we just decided that we all wanted to play at my house so I got a brainy idea!

I think all my friends should wait with me at the pickup line, and when Mommy pulls up I can just ask her *before* they get in the van with us.

This way I'm asking her *before* I have friends over.

Momma will be happy that I thought of all this. She said she likes when I used my head.

When Momma drove up, she gave me the stink eye when I asked her if all my friends could come over to our house to play with Skippy and Snickerdoodle.

She didn't think it was a good idea to come to our house now, but she had the smarty idea to meet later at the park!

That seemed fine with all of them 'cause I noticed they were smiling when we drove away.

Momma decided to remind me what asking "before" means.

"Ok, now tell me, how was your day, Ellie?" Momma asked me, but I couldn't pay attention to Mommy 'cause I was too busy looking for them puppies.

"Where are they? Where are them puppies, Momma?" I asked her 'cause I need to know.

"At home in their crate," she told me.

"They're probably crying since there's nobody there with

them!" I yelled, 'cause I couldn't stand the thought of it!

"It's all right. Your daddy is home with them, Ellie. Don't worry," she told me.

I felt better, but then I realized that if Daddy was home, then why were them puppies in their crate?

"Your daddy is working at home today and just put them in their crate when it was time for me to leave to pick you up," she said.

That made me feel better.

"Daddy has some very exciting news that he learned at his job today. He came home early so he could tell us about it, and then we are going out to eat to celebrate!" she said.

"McDonalds! Are we going to McDonalds?" I asked her, 'cause I just love that Ronald McDonald and his french fries.

"No, we're not going to McDonalds tonight, Ellie," Momma told me. "We'll let Daddy choose since it's his special night."

"Does he know about the Happy Meals, Momma? 'Cause there is nothing in this whole world that makes a night more special than a Happy Meal!" I explained.

"Yes, Happy Meals do mark an occasion, but I think we'll let Daddy choose," Mommy said as we pulled into our driveway.

I couldn't wait to get out of the van and see them sweet puppies!

So I ran up our sidewalk and through the front door in just twelve seconds.

I know 'cause I counted.

"Skippy! Snickerdoodle! I'm home!" I shouted, 'cause I couldn't wait to see those little balls of fur!

"They're in here!" Daddy yelled from the family room.

Momma says they call it the "family room" 'cause it's where the family spends the most time.

I'm not sure how they got the name for the "living room."

Daddy was on the floor playing with them puppies, and they were busy kissing him.

When they saw me, they ran right over to me 'cause they had kisses for me too!

"Hi there, little fellas! How are you my sweet, puppy wuppies?" I asked.

Those puppies must have had ants in their pants, 'cause they were jumping all over me!

"Where's my hello?" Daddy asked, and he had a big frown on his face, but he was just pretending to have his feelings hurt.

I put my arms around him and gave him a quick kiss so I could get back to them puppies.

Daddy said he had to talk to us about something, and to bring Skippy and Snickerdoodle over to the table so we could have a family meeting.

The only time we have a family meeting is when Mommy and Daddy want to add something to the family rules.

It's usually after I've done something that isn't acceptable, but I know I've been acceptable, so this should be interesting.

"Ellie, I have some big news! Something very exciting happened to me today. It's something that I've been working toward where I work. They offered me a job as a Travel Reporter," Daddy told me.

"So, you'll report the travel?" I asked, 'cause it didn't make any sense. I found that sometimes, parents don't make sense the first time they tell you something, so you just have to wait and let them try again.

"Well, what I'll be doing is traveling around the world and reporting my experiences on a TV show," he told me.

WAIT A MINUTE! DID HE JUST SAY TV SHOW?

T is for television.

"You're going to be on TV?" I asked him.
"That's right," he said, and he smiled real big.

"That TV?" I asked, pointing to our TV.

"That TV and TV's all around the world, honey," he said.

"So I'm going to be able to watch you on TV?" I asked, 'cause I thought the week was already great since we got the new puppies and all, but now Daddy was going to be on TV too!

What would MiShaun say about that?

"We haven't told you the best part, Ellie," Mommy said. "We're going to travel with your father!"

"Wow, we get to go! What about them puppies?" I asked while Skippy and Snickerdoodle sat on my lap and kept trying to lick my face.

"My boss was very kind and said that since Skippy and Snickerdoodle are family now, they will get to come too," Daddy said.

"What about school, Mommy? Will we go when I have my vacations?" I asked as the puppies wiggled in my lap.

"Yes, when you have your vacations and during the school year too. You will have a tutor," Mommy told me as she took Skippy off my lap.

"A tutor?" I asked, 'cause I never heard that word before.

"A tutor is someone that helps with school work. She will travel with us to make sure you don't fall behind in your studies," Momma said.

"It's okay if I fall behind, Momma. I can get my homework when I get back," I told her. "Remember when I had the stomach yuckies and stayed home from school for a bunch of days?"

"Well, this is a little different, Ellie," Daddy told me. "We're

going to be gone for long periods of time."

Daddy said that I wouldn't be going to school for about a year. He said that instead I would be going on vacations with Mommy, Daddy, and the puppies, and he wanted to know if that was okay.

Well, yeah, I'd say that is okay with me!

"When do we go? I'm ready!" I told him as I put Snickerdoodle back on the floor, 'cause he was getting too

wiggly and needed to get on the floor to get his wiggles out.

"We have to arrange everything, so you'll still go to school for a week or two while we set everything up. We also got you a fun gift!" he said as he handed me a purple box with a red bow!

I can't believe I get a present too! When I opened the box there was a video camera inside! And guess what? It's a purple video camera!

"We'll teach you how to use it because we want you to do a video diary while we're on our trips," he said.

I love presents, and this new purple video camera is a great present! Daddy knows that purple is one of my favoritest colors on account of it being my Nannie's favoritest color.

Nannie is my daddy's mommy and I love her.

"I get to make movies?" I asked. "Yay!"

"It's my understanding that it will be part of the work you'll be required to do for school," Daddy said. "We can learn how to use it later tonight."

"I just make movies of what I do all day?" I asked, 'cause this sounded like a whole lotta fun all at once.

"Yes, that's right," Daddy told me as he fiddled with the camera.

"And I make the movies every day?" I asked, just to be sure.

"Yes, Ellie, every day," he answered.

"So, we go on vacation, and I get to bring Skippy and Snickerdoodle, and I have a new video camera, and I don't go to school?" I asked.

This sounded like someone was pulling my leg, except Mommy says no one really pulls your leg. It's just another one of those parent sayings that makes my life so confusing.

"So, what's the catch?" I asked her.

"What's the catch?" Momma said, and she was laughing when she said it.

"Yep, the catch," I answered.

"There's no catch, honey. It's just a great opportunity for our family to travel while I work," Daddy said. "We'll make sure that you get all your studies done, because school is very important."

"Is that okay?" Momma asked.

"Oh YES!" I shouted, and then I jumped around the kitchen.

The puppies started barking at my crazy behavior, 'cause they'd never seen me like this before.

"Where are we going first, Daddy?" I asked him.

"The very first place we will be going is Arizona," he said.

"Arizonia?" I asked, 'cause I never heard of Arizonia.

"It's pronounced Arizona," he said.

"Arizonia," I said.

"Arizona," he repeated.

"Oh, Arizonia," I said.

"No, it's Arizona," he said.

"Why don't we go to Ohio? I know how to say Ohio," I told him as I plopped down on the couch.

"You'll get it. Just try it again, it's Ar-i-zon-a," Daddy said.

"Arizona," I repeated.

"There you go!" he said and he gave me a high five.

"Yay, when do we go to Arizonia?" I asked and then covered my mouth with my hands, 'cause I knew I said it wrong again!

He laughed and shook his head.

"Soon honey, but you don't have to wait to start your video diary," Daddy told me. "Mommy made this for you to have at the beginning of your first video."

Daddy handed me a pretty piece of purple cardboard that had flowers along the bottom. It said, "Ellie Carmichael goes to Arizona."

"Thanks, Mommy!" I told her. "Umm, would it be okay if I changed it a little? Is that okay? Can I change it?"

"Of course," she said as she handed me the package of markers.

I got a black magic marker and crossed off "Carmichael" and asked Daddy for help.

"Daddy, would you please write Adventure over the word Carmichael?" I asked him and handed him the magic marker.

Ellie ~~Carmichael~~ Adventure
Goes to Arizona

"May I ask why?" Daddy asked.

"It's just 'cause I'm going to be going on all these fun adventures and I thought the word 'adventure' would sound so much more, um, adventurous! Wait, is that a word, Daddy?" I asked him.

"Of course, that makes sense," Daddy said and he kissed the top of my head. "And yes, adventurous is a word."

I took my poster and camera, and skipped down the hall to my room, 'cause I was so excited about all this fun news!

Skippy and Snickerdoodle came running down the hall after me, and they were barking like crazy the whole way!

I guess they were happy about the big news, too!

# Chapter Ten

## Saying Goodbye!

Today, I get to have a party at school to say goodbye to all my friends! I get to bring mini cupcakes and juice boxes, and I even get to bring my puppies to class for ten whole minutes!

Ten minutes!

"Is it time yet?" Lori asked, as she tapped her pencil on her desk.

She started asking me this morning, and has been asking all day long, on account of her being super excited about them puppies coming!

"No, Mrs. Norris said the little hand needs to be on the two, and the big hand needs to be on the six," I told her. "So I think that means at two-sixty."

"That doesn't sound right. I just hope it's soon," Lori said.

"How come you have to go?" Dana asked, all sad-like. "Can't your dad just go and you stay here?"

"I want to go," I told her. "I'm going to miss you, but it's going to be fun going to all kinds of new places with them puppies."

"How do you know that they want to go, Ellie So Smelly?" MiShaun asked as she walked over to my desk.

She had her hands on her hips like she was mad or something.

"Maybe they don't want to go. Did you ask them?" MiShaun said.

"Um, no but that's just 'cause them puppies don't even know anything about trips," I told her. "And 'sides, they're little puppies! They don't know about much more than licking faces and wagging their tails."

"Instead of *them* puppies, Ellie, you should have said, *those* puppies in that sentence. Do you understand?" Mrs.

Norris asked as she walked over. "And MiShaun, do not refer to Ellie in that manner. We don't call people names."

I looked over at MiShaun, and she looked sad since she got in trouble with Mrs. Norris.

"I'm sure you know what is expected of you right now," Mrs. Norris said to MiShaun.

"I'm sorry, Ellie," she said with a big frowny on her face.

"That's okay. I forgive you," I told her. "Let's just get ready for them...I mean, those puppies!"

All my school friends started yelling and clapping their hands!

"Class, quiet please," Mrs. Norris said with her finger up to her lip.

Lori and Dana looked at me and we all smiled our biggest smiles, 'cause we knew she was going to give us good news.

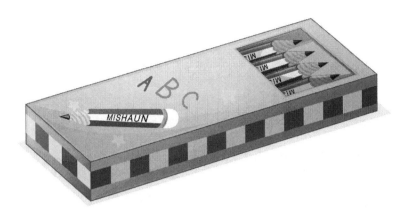

"In a few minutes we're going to have our going away party for Ellie," she said, but all the kids started clapping again before she even finished saying it.

"Yay!" Dillion said as he jumped around.

"I know we're all very excited for the party, but we have to get ready first. I need you to get up, quietly, and prepare your backpacks for the end of the day," Mrs. Norris told the class.

"Is it almost time to go home?" MiShaun asked. "I have to make sure I put my brand new red striped pencils away if it's time to go home."

MiShaun got brand new red striped pencils that have her name on them. She won't let anyone else use them, 'cause she says that we can't use them unless our name's MiShaun. I say that's just a tricky way not to share her brand new red striped pencils.

"Yes, please pack your backpacks for the end of the day and hurry, because our visitors will be here soon," Mrs. Norris told us as she erased the white board.

Just then, there was a knock on the door. It was my mommy and daddy with them puppies!

"It's finally time," Lori said, clapping her hands. "I can't wait to see the puppies!"

"Welcome! Please come in," Mrs. Norris said. "Ellie, would you like to help?"

"Would I?" I shouted, 'cause of course I want to help. I always want to help, even if there are no puppies. I just like to help!

"Please take the leashes and walk the puppies down the line so the students can take a minute with them," she told me. Mommy and Daddy started putting a mini cupcake and a juice box on each desk. The puppies were jumping up and down and wagging their tails. They seemed really excited about meeting all my friends.

"Wow, they sure are fluffy!" Keaton said as he bent down to pet them. He got a kiss from Snickerdoodle.

"I think this one likes me," Heather said when Skippy jumped up on her leg.

"He probably remembers me, right Ellie?" MiShaun said when Skippy ran over to her. "We're already close friends."

"I think we should take off their leashes, and then they can run around," I said, as I unhooked them. They took off like they had super powerful batteries in their legs! All the kids started running around to play with them, which made them start to bark, and now it was really a party!

"What happened?" Mrs. Norris asked as she ran after Snickerdoodle. "How'd they get off their leashes?"

I watched Skippy as he ran over to where Mommy and

Daddy had the box of cupcakes.

"Mommy!" I shouted as I pointed to the cupcakes. "Watch out!"

Mommy looked up and started moving toward the cupcakes, but Skippy beat her to it.

Skippy spied those mini cupcakes on the chair and

stood up on his furry back legs and used his paw to flip the box over. The cupcakes landed on the floor, and he was eating them in big gulps.

GULP!

GULP!

GULP!

Those cupcakes were quickly disappearing. He didn't even bother taking off the wrappers!

Snickerdoodle ran over and was licking the icing off the box when Daddy tried to grab him.

"Those will make them sick!" Mommy shouted. "Grab them, quick!"

When Daddy reached out for Skippy, Skippy thought he was playing and ran. Skippy turned around and gave Daddy one snappy bark before he darted between the desks behind him.

Snickerdoodle wanted to get in on the game too, so he

ducked when Daddy tried to grab him. He ran around Daddy and over to the bean bag that Mrs. Norris sits on when she reads to us. He was barking the whole time.

When Snickerdoodle barks, it just makes Skippy bark, so Skippy was barking too as they chased each other around the bean bag!

There was a whole lot of barking going on, and Mommy and Daddy were running around the classroom just trying to catch puppies!

Everybody in the class was loving it!

"I got one!" Trevor shouted, as he pulled Skippy up off the floor and held him up.

Skippy was twisting back and forth trying to get free. He bent his body around and started licking Trevor's hand, which made Trevor giggle and drop him.

Luckily, Mommy caught Skippy before he hit the floor!

"Got you!" she said. Momma was breathing really hard, but she was still smiling.

Her smile went away though when she saw Snickerdoodle running toward the door.

"Close that door, please!" Mrs. Norris shouted, but Snickerdoodle was already out the door and running down the hall.

Daddy disappeared and then came back a minute later with a wiggly Snickerdoodle in his hands.

"I think we need to rename this one Wiggles," Daddy said as Mommy put the leash back on Snickerdoodle.

"Wiggles...I like that name!" I shouted.

"No, honey, Daddy is just joking," Momma told me.

"Okay, I'll have to remember the name Wiggles for our next pet," I told her.

"Let's hold off on naming our next pet since we just got Skippy and Snickerdoodle, and I think Skippy and Snickerdoodle should say goodbye for now. Daddy will take them to the van, and I'll take care of this mess," Mommy said.

Mrs. Norris had her hands up, and she was shaking her head.

Momma wasn't happy when she looked at the mess the puppies made in the classroom.

There was a big pile of squished cupcakes on the carpet.

"What do we say to Mr. and Mrs. Carmichael for bringing in the puppies?" Mrs. Norris asked as she opened the door for Daddy to leave.

# THANK YOU!

We all yelled "thank you" at the same time. They taught us that in kindergarten, but I still remember it in the first grade.

"Ellie, the class has a gift for you," Mrs. Norris told me as she motioned for me to come to the front of the classroom.

I sure love gifts, so I was super happy!

Keaton gave me a card that had a beautiful rainbow on it. "We all signed it," he said as he handed me the card.

When I opened it some stamps fell to the floor.

"We gave you stamps so you could send us postcards of all the places you visit. We'll keep track of your travels by pinning your postcards to our map of the United States," Mrs. Norris said.

"Thank you," I told her. "I don't know how to write that good-ly yet, or well-ly."

"You're welcome, and it's well, not "good-ly" or "well-ly," Mrs. Norris told me. "I'm sure your mother or father can help you write out your postcards."

"Here's another gift," Dana said. "It's the best one," she whispered as she gave it to me.

I opened the box, and it had a stuffed bear inside!

"Oh wow!" I shouted, 'cause I was so happy with my gift.

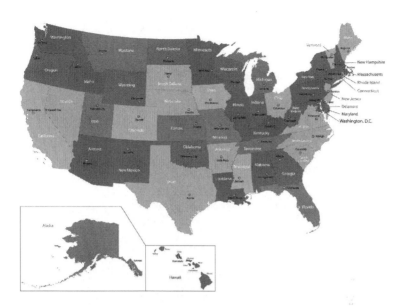

"I just love this stuffed bear!"

"It's just like our school mascot, Billy the Bear," Mrs. Norris said. "If you miss us, just hug your stuffed animal and know that it's from us."

I was so happy that they got me this stuffed bear!

"Thank you, everybody!" I told them. "I will send you postcards and tell you how the puppies are doing."

Just then, the bell rang for us to leave for the day. I put my backpack on and squeezed my stuffed bear tight.

As I got in line to leave for the day, I thought about how lucky I was to get to go on trips with my family and how lucky I was to have all these great friends.

"Thank you everybody! I love my gifts and will miss you," I shouted as I left my classroom and waved goodbye to all my classmates.

I gave Billy another squeeze and whispered into his

133

brown ear, "I'm so glad I get to bring you with me on my first trip to Arizonia!"

I gotta remember to tell Skippy and Snickerdoodle that Billy isn't a toy. As long as they remember that, we'll have a great trip!

It's time to say goodbye to all my school friends for now and Arizonia...I mean, Arizona, here we come!

The End

# Check for understanding

Do you remember what you read? Try this test to see what you remember!

1. What did Lori and Dana want instead of a puppy?
   a. turtles
   b. ponies
   c. tigers

2. What did Ellie do in her room that got her in trouble?
   a. raised rabbits
   b. painted the walls and got some on the carpet
   c. put stickers on her closet door

3. What did Ellie's mother call the woman who walked lots of dogs?
   a. a dog walker
   b. Estelle
   c. probably very tired

4. What was the name of the adoption boutique?
   a. Adopt-a-lot
   b. Pete's Puppy Place
   c. Puppy Play Pen

5. What was the name of the lady at the barn where they adopted the puppies?
   a. Talulah
   b. Kitty
   c. Izzie

6. What woke up the first puppy on his first night in his crate?
   a. a tummy ache
   b. the ice cream truck
   c. an alarm clock

7. What are the puppies' middle names?
   a. Marshmella and Cotton Candy
   b. Stinky and Pinky
   c. Twinky and Brownie

8. Who is Ellie named after?
   a. her grandmother
   b. the puppies
   c. her teacher

9. What happened to MiShaun at the park?
   a. she lost her sandwich
   b. she swallowed a bug
   c. she lost a tooth

BONUS QUESTION:

10. The first trip will be to the state of Arizona. What is the
    state nickname?
    a. The Super Hot State
    b. The Cactus State
    c. The Grand Canyon State

# Answer Key

How did you do? Check here!

1. b
2. b
3. a
4. c
5. b
6. c
7. a
8. a
9. c
10. c

# Thanks

I couldn't have written this book without the encouragement of my family, especially my father, my husband, and my children.

Thank you to my husband, Dean, who is always there for me whenever I need him. He took selected vector art and, magically, made it fit the characters in my story. He also helped make the cover exactly how I had envisioned it!

Ryan and Matty, you are my life! I am so lucky to be the mother of such amazing kids. Thanks for all your help with the book and for all your love.

To John Ewing, a former Disney illustrator and a wonderful friend, it was amazing working with you to bring Skippy and Snickerdoodle to life. Your many talents continue to inspire me.

Thank you also to John and Martha Dougherty, Susan, Ron, and Michael for their love, and for being there always for us. We love you.

# About the Author

"Ellie Adventure Picking Out Puppies" was written after Colleen Dougherty's youngest son asked her to write a book about puppies. They had just added two puppies to their family, so material for the book was literally running around her feet! Colleen put her current writing project aside, and got to work on the Ellie Adventure series. The title character is named after her maternal grandmother and some of the lines delivered by Ellie came straight from things her sons have said. Colleen Dougherty lives in Chandler, Arizona with her husband Dean, her two sons, her two dogs and at least one foster dog or litter of foster puppies.

# Reviews - The silent applause

Ebook customers:

In a moment, Kindle will ask you if you'd like to leave a rating for "Ellie Adventure Picking Out Puppies." I would really appreciate it if you could leave a review on my book page. If you liked the book, a review acts as a silent applause and means a great deal to an author like me! You may even read your reviews on the back cover of a future book!

If you'd like to reach me by email, please do! I can be reached at:

theellieadventure@gmail.com

If you would like to be notified when my second book "Ellie Adventure Grand Canyon Puppies" will be available for purchase, please fill out the Contact Form on my website:

www.colleendougherty.com

Best to you always, Colleen

Disclaimer

This is a work of fiction that makes adopting a pet seem like lots of fun, which it is, but it's also lots of work. If Ellie's experiences with adopting a dog appealed to you, please research available animals to determine which breed would be best for your family. Adopting a pet is a lifetime commitment.

Seven years ago, after losing our beloved dog Buster to cancer, we bought two puppies from a breeder because we didn't realize that we could get dogs that my husband would not be allergic to through adoption. We now know that pretty much all breeds are available to adopt through a local animal shelter or foster group. As of this writing, my family has fostered a female dog in need and, separately, a litter of five puppies through the foster group, One Dog Arizona. All of the precious animals that have gone through our house as fosters have been adopted into loving homes. We currently have four puppies, from two different litters, that we're fostering.

Please consult your local shelter or foster group if you would like information on adopting a pet. Adopting a pet is a huge commitment that needs to be taken seriously. Please don't enter into an adoption agreement lightly.

DON'T SHOP

ADOPT

DON'T COT

AДOПT

ФЛЕХАЙК

СОК

АБСОРПТIO

СЫСТИМ

KOX

BOЛ

OH

ДИМАНД

АБВГДЕЁЖЗ

ОФ

ТВ

МИНЮ

ПОПКОРН

ПОП

КОРН

АРИЗОНА

МОММЫ

70578991R00088

Made in the USA
Columbia, SC
09 May 2017